Pooch Parlour

V.I.P.

(Very Important Pup!)

For Simon – KC

For CB and AA, with much
appreciation x – JAD

STRIPES PUBLISHING
An imprint of Little Tiger Press
1 The Coda Centre, 189 Munster Road,
London SW6 6AW

This paperback edition first published
in Great Britain in 2014.

ISBN: 978-1-84715-428-6

A CIP catalogue record for this book is available
from the British Library.

Printed and bound in the UK.

2 4 6 8 10 9 7 5 3 1

V.I.P.
(Very Important Pup!)

Katy Cannon

Stripes

Chapter One

"Lulu, we're here!" Abi bounced on her toes as she looked up at the powder-blue door with the words "Pooch Parlour" curling above it in silver letters. "We're really here!"

At her side, Lulu the bichon frise beat her fluffy white tail excitedly against the pavement.

"Should we just go in, do you think?" Abi asked. There was a sign on the door saying "All Dogs Welcome", but there was also one saying "Closed".

Before Abi could decide, Lulu pushed her head against the door, making the bell attached to it chime.

"I guess we're going in!" Abi laughed.

Inside, Pooch Parlour was everything Abi had dreamed it would be. This was her first visit since Aunt Tiffany had moved the parlour to a bigger space in central London.

She'd seen photos online, but they didn't show the pictures of celebrities and their dogs on the walls, or the glass cases displaying every colour of grooming brush, all with sparkly diamonds in the handles.

"Abi, darling. You found us!" Aunt Tiffany appeared through a shimmering curtain behind the reception desk. "So sorry I had to rush off this morning. There's a lot to do before we open for the day! But now I'm all yours, until our first client arrives."

Abi smiled at her aunt as she bent down to unclip Lulu's lead. "That's OK. It *is* only just round the corner." In fact, she could almost see Pooch Parlour from the window of her candy-striped guest bedroom, but Aunt Tiffany had still drawn her a map showing exactly how to get from her flat to the parlour.

When Abi's parents had first told her that she'd be spending the whole summer with Aunt Tiffany, while they were away in America, she'd been nervous. She'd never spent so long apart from her mum and dad before. But Lulu had bumped her head against Abi's hand as if to say, *You'll still have me. We'll be OK*, and Abi realized that as long as she had Lulu with her, she'd never be lonely.

And *then* she'd remembered Pooch Parlour and forgotten to be nervous altogether. A whole summer at Aunt Tiffany's glamorous luxury dog-grooming salon sounded like far too much fun to waste time worrying!

Abi and her mum had filled her best backpack with clothes, and they'd packed all of Lulu's favourite toys in her own bag. And then, yesterday, the day had finally come! Mum and Dad had dropped her off at Aunt Tiffany's, and

Abi had hugged and kissed them, too excited to be upset about saying goodbye.

At the flat, Abi and Lulu were welcomed by Aunt Tiffany and Hugo, her miniature dachshund, who'd been wearing his very best tartan dressing gown!

As if he knew Abi was thinking of him, Hugo padded under the shiny pink curtain, dressed today in a stripy blue and white jumper that matched the one Aunt Tiffany was wearing. Lulu gave an excited woof when she spotted him and dashed over to press her nose up against his side. Hugo gave a doggy sigh and stared at Abi with big eyes.

"Sorry, Hugo," Abi said, with a shrug. "She likes you."

Aunt Tiffany laughed, high and tinkling. "He likes her too, really. Lulu's a lively one."

At the sound of her name, Lulu looked up and barked.

"Dad calls her a bouncy cloud on legs," Abi said, stroking Lulu's head.

"Bichon frises are very fluffy dogs," Aunt Tiffany agreed. "She must take a lot of grooming."

"Every six to eight weeks," Abi said. She'd read up on the best way to look after Lulu before she'd even been allowed to take her home. "Mum does it herself."

They were a doggy family, Mum always said. Dad wrote books about dogs – and he'd been invited on a book tour to talk about them in bookshops and pet shops all over America that summer. Mum, who was a vet specializing in looking after dogs and puppies, had gone with him, but they'd decided that Abi would have more fun staying with Aunt Tiffany. They'd promised to call her every night while they were away and Abi couldn't wait to talk to them that evening. She'd be able to tell them all about her first day at Pooch Parlour. She wondered how many dogs she'd get to meet...

Abi loved dogs more than anything, and she loved Lulu most of all! When she grew up, she planned to work with animals, just like her parents. But not to write about them, or look after them when they were sick. Abi wanted to work with animal actors — the dogs and cats and other pets that starred in some of her favourite TV shows and films. She had a feeling that a whole summer at Pooch Parlour would be fantastic practice!

Aunt Tiffany tilted her head to study Lulu. "Your mum does a great job of grooming Lulu," she said, reaching down to pet the fluffy white dog. "But how do you think Lulu would like to have a proper Pooch Parlour makeover? After all, she has to look the part, if she's going to be a Parlour dog."

Abi's eyes widened and Lulu gave an excited bark. "She'd love it. And so would I!"

"Wonderful." Aunt Tiffany beamed and held open the shimmery pink curtain for them.

"We'll get Lulu into the spa, let her sniff our bubble baths, and see which one she likes best. After that, you can help me choose the perfect accessories for her. I've just got in a new range of glitter bows that I think you're going to love!"

Chapter Two

"We'll start in the Doggy Spa," Aunt Tiffany said, opening a door with a glittery sign on it. Lulu pushed her way through first, her little nose snuffling along the floor, following trails of scent.

Stepping into the room, Abi stopped and sniffed too. The air was filled with delicious smells, all mingling together. Abi gazed around

her at the Doggy Spa. It was certainly different
to washing Lulu in the bath at home and drying
her on a towel!

The room was decorated in calming blues
and greens, with tiny spotlights dotted all over
the ceiling. Soothing classical music played and
shelves full of bottles, all with neatly printed
labels, lined the walls. Round the edge of the

room were the grooming stations – tables with padded towelling cushions and baskets filled with the grooming supplies attached to each one. And in the centre of the room…

"Is that a bone-shaped bath?" Abi asked, looking down at the strangely shaped tub. Lulu barked excitedly as she hopped up the two steps leading into the bath and peered over the edge.

"A perfect doggy bath," Aunt Tiffany replied. "Now, the first thing Lulu needs to do is choose her bubbles."

Lulu looked like she might jump into the empty bathtub at any moment, so Abi stepped up to her and said, "Wait, Lulu." She smiled as the little dog did as she was told. "Good girl."

Aunt Tiffany walked over to the wall of bottles. Hands on her hips, she stared at them. "Hmm, now, what would be just right for Lulu?"

Abi stepped closer and peered at the bottles, reading the labels. There was "Barking Blossoms", "Fur Tree Forest", "Papaya Paws" and lots of others. Finally, Aunt Tiffany picked three bottles from the shelf and carried them over to the bath.

"Come, Lulu," Abi said, and Lulu hopped down the steps again and sat, tail patting the tiled floor.

Crouching down, Aunt Tiffany held each bottle and let Lulu sniff the bubbles inside. Then Lulu barked once and pushed her nose against the "Papaya Paws" bottle.

"Great choice!" Aunt Tiffany said. "That's one of my favourites."

Lulu looked very pleased with herself, and Abi laughed at the way she wagged her tail and shuffled around on the tiles, impatient to get into the bath.

With the water running, Aunt Tiffany handed Abi the bottle. "Do you want to pour it in? Just two capfuls."

Abi nodded and, taking the bottle, carefully measured out the right amount and poured it into the running water. Almost immediately the bath started to smell of tropical fruit and desert islands. This was definitely the most luxurious bath Lulu had ever had – in fact,

Abi wondered if Aunt Tiffany might have more of these bubbles at home for *her* to try!

Aunt Tiffany handed Abi a Pooch Parlour apron, just like hers, and Abi tied it round her waist. She felt like real Pooch Parlour staff now!

Lulu loved baths. As soon as Aunt Tiffany had brushed and combed out her coat and called for her to hop in, she flew straight into the bubbles, splashing and barking. Bits of foam and droplets of water flew everywhere, but Aunt Tiffany didn't seem to mind.

And when she started to rub the doggy shampoo into Lulu's fur, the little dog calmed down and stood still in the shallow water.

After her bath and shampoo – Aunt Tiffany
called it a "Sudsy Special" – it was time for
Lulu's blow-dry. Abi got to help, rubbing her
pet down with a super-fluffy towel, before Aunt
Tiffany combed through Lulu's thick coat again
and got out the Doggy Dryer to finish drying
her off. Then she picked up the grooming
scissors to give Lulu's coat a trim.

"Beautiful," Aunt Tiffany said, standing back
to admire her work.

Lulu barked with pride and, Abi had to admit,
her coat had never looked quite so gleaming
white before.

"And now for the fun bit!" Aunt Tiffany said.

"That wasn't the fun bit?" Abi asked, her
excitement rising. "Then what's next?"

"The wardrobe room!"

The wardrobe room was down the corridor and through two huge double doors.

"This is my absolutely favourite part of the whole parlour," Aunt Tiffany said. "Hugo's too." As she said his name, the little dachshund appeared beside them.

"It looks like Hugo thinks he's ready for a change of image," Abi laughed as Hugo plonked his bottom down next to Lulu's.

"Not now, Hugo." Aunt Tiffany opened the doors. "Today it's Lulu's turn for a makeover."

The room was set out like a clothes shop, with rails and racks of outfits, and accessories laid out by colour. The only difference was, these outfits were doggy-sized!

A lady with pale blonde hair in a ponytail, wearing the Pooch Parlour uniform, appeared from a curtained-off room.

"Hello," she said, smiling at them. "You

must be Abi and Lulu. I've heard so much about you from Tiffany. I'm Mel, the wardrobe assistant."

Abi smiled shyly and said hello, while Lulu went to sniff round Mel's ankles as her own way of saying hi.

Mel bent down and petted Lulu's head. "Aren't you a beauty?" she said, and Abi liked her immediately. "I bet we've got the perfect outfit for you here. Why don't you take a look, Abi? See what you think would look best on her."

It was so hard to choose! Abi wandered round the wardrobe room, running her fingers over dresses and sweaters and tutus and coats – even dressing gowns like Hugo had been wearing yesterday! They were all so lovely, but none of them seemed quite right for Lulu...

Then she spotted it – a purple T-shirt with lots of tiny ribbon bows in all sorts of colours sewn on. It was perfect!

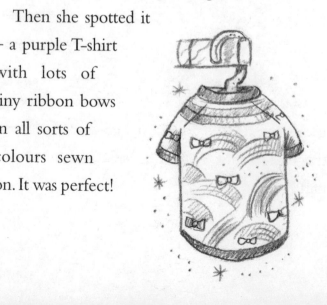

She looked over at Aunt Tiffany to see if she agreed. Aunt Tiffany nodded and gestured towards Mel.

"How about this one?" Abi asked Mel, holding it up.

Mel clapped her hands together and grinned. "It's lovely! Let's see what it looks like on."

"Wait a moment," Aunt Tiffany said. "It just needs…" Moving over to the accessories cabinets, she selected a glittery collar and a bright pink bow, and handed them to Mel.

Mel took the T-shirt as well and headed back towards the curtained-off area. "Come on, Lulu," she said. "Let's get you ready for your fashion show."

But before they could make it to the fitting room, the double doors opened again and Kim the receptionist walked in, followed by a very familiar lady…

Chapter Three

"I'm sorry to interrupt—" Kim began, but the lady beside her started talking at the same time.

"Tiffany! I'm sorry, I know you're so, so busy, but I need your help! It's an emergency!"

Aunt Tiffany smiled. "Now, Daisy, don't worry. Whatever it is, I'm sure we can fix it."

Abi tried not to stare. It was Daisy Lane. Daisy Lane, the star of the *Barking Mad* movies.

Abi loved those movies – she never imagined that she'd get to meet Daisy herself!

And if Daisy Lane was here… Abi looked down and spotted the tiny marmalade-coloured Pomeranian pressing up against Daisy's legs. It was Jade! With her bushy orange coat and foxy face, she might be an even bigger star than Daisy, Abi thought.

Abi had seen all the *Barking Mad* movies at least twice. First she persuaded her mum and dad to take her to see them at the cinema, usually with her best friend Emily. Then, when they came out on DVD, she'd ask for them as presents for birthdays and Christmas.

She and Emily knew lots of the lines off by heart and they would act out scenes in the playground at break time. Just wait until she told Emily she had actually met Daisy and Jade!

Aunt Tiffany took Daisy to sit down on one of the leather armchairs in the wardrobe room and sent Kim to fetch her a cup of herbal tea. Jade jumped up on to Daisy's lap, barking a little, and Daisy petted her until she settled down.

Mel popped the items they'd picked out for Lulu into the changing room.

"We'll finish Lulu's fashion makeover later," she whispered to Abi, with a smile.

"Now, Daisy," Aunt Tiffany said. "Why don't you tell me what's happened?"

"I just had a call from my old friend Kerri Kaye, presenter of *Limelight!*" Daisy said.

Abi's eyes widened. *Limelight!* was the biggest celebrity news show on TV. Emily's mum was a huge fan. She said that Kerri Kaye was the best entertainment reporter in the world. "Her co-host for tonight pulled out and she's asked me to fill the slot. They're pre-recording the show this afternoon to broadcast this evening. Normally I'd have said no at such short notice, but Kerri is such a great friend of mine, so…"

"So you said yes," Aunt Tiffany guessed. "Well, that doesn't sound so bad."

"Except I need to be at the studio in an hour, and Jade needs a bath and a brush, and she doesn't have a thing to wear! She needs an outfit to go with mine…" Daisy dug around in her handbag, unsettling Jade on her lap and making the tiny dog bark again. Pulling out a photo from her bag, Daisy said, "See? This is what I'm wearing. But Jade has nothing that matches!"

Aunt Tiffany took the photo from Daisy and smiled. "Well, that we can fix, can't we, Abi?"

"Yes, Aunt Tiffany," Abi said, hoping she wasn't blushing too much at being close to a real superstar. If Aunt Tiffany said they could, then they would!

Daisy peered at her, her hands smoothing down Jade's coat to try and soothe her. "I don't think we've met, have we?"

"This is my niece, Abi," Aunt Tiffany said. "She's here for the summer and I know she's going to be a huge help. She's great with dogs! That's her dog Lulu over there."

Daisy seemed to notice Lulu for the first time and her face brightened. "Oh, isn't she adorable! A bichon frise?"

Abi nodded. "She just had her first 'Sudsy Special' here this morning and she loved it!" The words came out in an excited rush.

"Yes, she did," Aunt Tiffany said. "Now, Daisy, Kim will take you back through to the waiting area for your tea and Hugo can keep you company. I'll take care of all Jade's grooming myself, to make sure she looks perfect for the cameras."

"Oh good," Daisy said, looking very relieved. "Thank you so much, Tiffany. I don't know what Jade and I would do without you!"

Daisy lifted Jade and put her on the floor, then stood up and headed after Kim. Jade started to follow, scurrying to keep up, with her plumed tail twitching.

"I'll be back soon, baby," Daisy said, kneeling down and blowing kisses to Jade. "You be good for Tiffany and Abi, now." Jade barked again, until Lulu approached and sniffed around the smaller dog, distracting her briefly as Daisy left.

When the door closed, Abi asked, "Do you think … could I help with Jade's grooming?"

"You most certainly can," Aunt Tiffany said. "Jade can be a tricky customer. And Pom Poms – Pomeranians – need a great deal of regular grooming. You can learn a lot by watching how I groom her. Besides, didn't you say you wanted to learn the tricks of the trade? This can be your first lesson: Always keep the clients happy!"

From what Aunt Tiffany and Daisy had said, Abi guessed that Jade had spent plenty of time at Pooch Parlour, but she still seemed nervous when they led her into the Doggy Spa. Was it just because Daisy wasn't with them? Some dogs did get nervous without their owners near, Abi knew. And Daisy and Jade were always together in interviews or photos!

Jade stayed by the door, padding anxiously round in a little circle. Abi sat cross-legged on the floor next to her and tried to remember

what her mum did with nervous dogs.

Keeping her voice calm and soft, Abi said, "Don't worry, Jade. Daisy is just in the next room. And won't she be pleased when she sees how lovely and clean you are?"

Jade stopped pacing and moved closer, and Abi smiled. Glancing up at Aunt Tiffany, she saw her aunt giving her a thumbs-up. It was working! Slowly, so as not to startle Jade, Abi ran her hand over the little Pom Pom's bushy coat, hoping it would soothe her. Soon, Jade seemed completely relaxed.

"Well done, Abi," Aunt Tiffany said. "I knew you'd be a big help. It'll be much easier to bathe and groom Jade now she's calm."

Abi grinned. Across the room, Lulu padded over to the shelves full of bottles, as if to say, *I know what happens next!*

Aunt Tiffany turned on the bath taps. "Abi, why don't you and Lulu choose three bottles for Jade to sniff while I brush out her coat?"

"OK," Abi agreed. Smiling at Jade, she got carefully to her feet – so as not to startle her – and walked over to Lulu.

Abi stared at the shelves. There were so many bottles to choose from! How could she know which ones Jade would like best? She really wanted to do a good job and show Aunt Tiffany what a help she could be at Pooch Parlour.

Abi thought back to what she knew about Jade from the interviews with Daisy that she'd read in *Animal Antics* magazine. She knew that Jade liked running in freshly cut grass, her favourite snacks were Barker's Bites, and … and that she loved it when Daisy bought roses for their apartment! Abi gathered three bottles from the shelf – one that smelled of summer meadows, one cookies-and-cream fragrance, and one rose-scented one.

As she took the lids off to let Jade sniff them, Aunt Tiffany smiled at her choices. "How did you know those three are her favourites?"

Abi shrugged, secretly pleased to have done so well. "I guess I just know dogs."

Aunt Tiffany took over for the actual bath, but she let Abi rub the doggy shampoo into Jade's coat. Jade fussed a bit, but Abi managed to keep her calm. Soaking wet, Jade's bushy coat was plastered to her skin, making her look much smaller.

Abi remembered how little Jade looked in the *Barking Mad* films beside all the bigger dogs. But she was always the smart one that managed to escape through a gap and find a sneaky way to beat the bad guys.

Abi helped with the fluff dry, with Lulu dancing round her feet, obviously remembering her own session with the towel earlier that day. Then Aunt Tiffany finished drying off Jade's thick coat with the Doggy Dryer, brushing it out thoroughly.

Once she was dry, Aunt Tiffany gave Jade a little trim, holding the dog still to make sure she didn't wriggle. "She doesn't need much off," she explained, as she snipped away. "It's not long since her last grooming session. But Pomeranian coats do grow fast! They actually have a double coat – see?" She held up Jade's straight overcoat for Abi to touch the thick, soft undercoat beneath. "It takes a lot of brushing and drying. Good job I had you to help me today!"

Finishing up, Aunt Tiffany said, "Right, time to choose your outfit, Miss Jade!"

"Do we need Daisy for this part?" Abi asked, as they left the Doggy Spa and headed for the wardrobe room.

Jade stuck close to Abi, but she knew the dog would be calmer if Daisy was there. Lulu padded alongside Jade, like a fluffy white big sister, and the little Pom Pom skittered across the corridor, as if she didn't know whether to be friends or run away.

Aunt Tiffany shook her head. "Daisy has given me a photo of her own outfit for the show," she reminded Abi, handing the picture over. "All we need to do is find Jade something that complements it."

Abi stared at the picture. Daisy's dress was a shimmering gold, almost the same colour as

Jade's fur. The wardrobe room at Pooch Parlour was big, but did they have anything to match?

Throwing open the double doors, Aunt Tiffany called, "Mel?"

There was no reply.

Kim stuck her head through the other door, the one that led to reception. "She's popped out with Mrs Travers," she said. "You know, to help choose the clothes for the fashion show…"

Aunt Tiffany groaned. "Of course. Oh well, Abi and I will have to manage on our own."

As Kim closed the door, Abi heard Daisy calling, "Kim? Could I get another cup of tea?"

Jade barked at the sound of her owner's voice, so Abi led her over to the other side of the room, trying to distract her with the shiny bows and collars in the accessories cabinet. But Jade kept glancing back at the door.

"Where to start…" Aunt Tiffany was moving

towards the rail full of party outfits when her mobile phone rang. "Hello? Oh, hello, Don. Of course! We're very excited to be involved. Hang on, the file is just in my office. Give me one moment" – she put her hand over the phone and turned to Abi – "Right, do you want to make a start looking at outfits for Jade, while I deal with this? I'll be back as soon as I can."

Lulu pressed up against her leg, and Abi knew she was saying, *I'll help!*

Abi nodded. "Of course I can, Aunt Tiffany!" She stared at the rails and racks of clothing. The perfect outfit had to be in there somewhere, right? If she could find it on her own, Aunt Tiffany was sure to be impressed.

Chapter Five

As the door shut behind Aunt Tiffany, Abi took a deep breath and tried to decide where to start. She looked at the photo again, taking in the gold fabric and the bright blue jewellery. Then she looked at Jade. The Pom Pom's sharp little eyes stared back, waiting to see what Abi was going to do next.

"Right then," Abi said, just like Aunt Tiffany always did. "We need something in gold or bright blue, in just the right size for a Pomeranian. How hard can that be?"

Jade padded over to the rack nearest the door and yapped a few times.

"And apparently we're starting here!" Abi laughed. At least trying things on might help Jade forget that Daisy wasn't there. Joining the Pom Pom at the rack, Abi began to flick through the outfits. "Hmm, this might work," she said, picking out a gold sequinned jacket with matching collar.

But Jade had moved over to investigate the door, pawing at the wood. Abi led her back to the next rack, where she found another gold collar, and a waistcoat. They matched Daisy's dress, she supposed, but Abi couldn't shake the feeling that they still weren't quite right.

She looked at the outfits again, then at Jade, and realized the problem. How could Jade wear a tight-fitting outfit over that bushy, fluffy coat?

"Sorry, Jade. Not those ones. But there has to

46

be something here that works," she muttered, putting the clothes back on the rails.

Lulu pressed her head against Abi's leg and she looked down at her doggy pal.

"Found something, Lulu?"

With a bark, Lulu bounded off towards the other end of the wardrobe. Curious, Abi followed.

Lulu paused in front of a rack of doggy costumes. Abi saw fairy outfits, bee outfits, dinosaur outfits … all kinds of wonderful costumes! But they weren't right for *Limelight!*

"Sorry, Lulu. Not for today." But then Abi spotted another rack just behind it, filled with dresses that looked like they belonged on the red carpet. There had to be something here!

"Now we're getting closer," Abi said, looking at the two dogs excitedly.

It didn't take long for Abi to find the perfect thing – a gold collar with a flowing cape attached, in the exact same shade of sapphire-blue as Daisy's jewellery!

"What do you think?" Abi asked, holding it up. Jade sniffed at the material, and barked her approval. "Then let's see how it looks."

Kneeling down, Abi placed the cloak over Jade's back, fastening the collar around her neck. She looked fabulous! Even Jade seemed to think so – she started turning in circles, admiring the shiny blue of her cape.

"And now for the finishing touches!" Abi

said, skipping over to another stand to collect something that had caught her eye. Aunt Tiffany – and Daisy – were going to be amazed!

Aunt Tiffany met Abi at the wardrobe room door and looked surprised when Abi said they were finished. But then she saw Jade and said, "She looks perfect. Let's go and show Daisy!"

Kim was sitting with Daisy in reception. Both women stopped talking as Abi walked in, leading Jade. Nervously, she stepped aside to give Jade centre stage...

"Oh!" Daisy clapped her hands together, eyes wide, as she took in Jade's outfit, including the bright blue, sequinned beret that matched her cape. "It's perfect! It's absolutely, wonderfully perfect!" Holding her hands out towards Jade, she said, "Come here, my beautiful!"

With a little yap, Jade bounded towards her owner and jumped up into Daisy's lap.

"I'm so glad you like it," Abi said, relief making her feel so light that she couldn't keep a beaming smile from her face.

"And it was all Abi's work," Aunt Tiffany said, looking proud. "She has a real talent with animals. She kept Jade wonderfully calm in the Doggy Spa too."

Suddenly, all Daisy's attention was on Abi, making her squirm, just a bit. "So, do you want to work here with your aunt when you're older?"

"Um, maybe. But actually, my dream is to work with animals in films and TV shows."

"Really?" Daisy said thoughtfully. Then she grinned. "In that case, I insist you all come with me to the filming this afternoon! Abi, you can look after Jade while I'm in make-up."

Chapter Six

Daisy's car was waiting for them outside.

"You go ahead with the dogs," Daisy told Abi, motioning them towards the door. "I just need to pay for all Jade's treats."

She held up the bag containing Jade's outfit for the filming. They'd decided to take it off until they were ready to film, to make sure it didn't get dirty.

Abi clipped glittery leads on to Lulu, Hugo and Jade's collars and led them out on to the pavement. She had to go back for Jade when the little Pom Pom tried to run over to Daisy instead.

Outside, Abi blinked, staring at Daisy's car. It was the pinkest, longest limousine she could ever have imagined. "I guess famous people don't take the bus," she said to the dogs, as the driver came round and opened the door for them, like Abi was a film star!

Jade jumped in first, using the special doggy step the driver provided. She obviously felt at home in the luxury of the limo, as she headed straight for a velvet dog bed. Lulu bounced in after Jade and set about exploring everything, while Hugo was a little slower, stopping to sniff the seats cautiously.

Abi stepped inside and took a seat near the dogs. Jade was tucking into some Barker's Bites in a shiny silver bowl. She seemed much calmer now she was in a familiar place, with her favourite things, even though Daisy wasn't there. Abi decided she'd ask Daisy if she could take some of Jade's treats into the studio with them, in case she needed something to calm her down while Daisy was getting ready.

Lulu and Hugo nuzzled close to Jade, obviously hoping that the Pomeranian might share, but she didn't!

Abi's mobile phone buzzed and she pulled it out of her pocket. Seeing she had a message from her best friend Emily, Abi grinned and read it quickly.

How's the doggy parlour? it said. *Met any celebrities yet?*

Abi giggled. Emily had no idea how close to the truth she was! Quickly, she tapped a text back. Her parents had given her the mobile for emergencies, but she was allowed to use the free texts to keep in touch with Emily.

It's incredible! Daisy Lane and Jade came in this morning. Now I'm going to the TV studio with them! I'll fill you in later.

The car door opened and Aunt Tiffany and Daisy stepped in – Emily would have to wait to find out more. Abi slipped her phone back in her pocket.

"Jade, darling. We have to share our treats with our friends," Daisy said, as she sat down and the limo started to move.

Jade looked up, but then went straight back to her bowl. Lulu and Hugo turned matching sad, hungry eyes on Daisy.

Daisy sighed. "There are more biscuits in that cupboard just beside you, Abi. Would you mind getting them, please?"

Abi looked for a cupboard, but all she could see were the smooth panels of the car walls. Then she spotted what looked like the outline of a door. She pressed the edge and it sprung open, revealing silver tins with the luxury doggy biscuit label on them, and several more silver bowls.

Lulu was already sitting at her feet, looking up hopefully. Hugo came and nuzzled up against her legs, and Abi couldn't help but smile.

They were such a pair already, and Lulu had only been there a day! She wished that Jade could make friends as easily as Hugo and Lulu had. It would make looking after her at the studio much easier.

Abi tipped a few biscuits into the bowl and set it in front of Lulu and Hugo. "Not too many," she said firmly. She turned to Daisy and bit her lip. It felt so weird to ask a celebrity for something. "I was wondering, do you think I could take some biscuits for Jade while we're at the studio?"

Daisy nodded. "That's a very good idea. Sometimes she needs a bit of a distraction when I'm away."

"Great." Abi grabbed a small snack bag of Barker's Bites from the cupboard.

"Good thinking, Abi," Aunt Tiffany whispered to her, and Abi felt very pleased with herself.

Abi's phone buzzed again in her pocket, but she didn't answer it. Mum would have said it was very bad manners to check her phone in front of a celebrity!

But Daisy said, "Is that your phone? I don't mind if you need to answer it."

Abi shook her head. "It's OK. It's just my best friend Emily. We're keeping in touch by text while I'm away this summer."

"That's nice. Is Emily going to come and visit you at Pooch Parlour?" Daisy asked.

Abi looked up. "She'd like to. But I haven't asked Aunt Tiffany yet…"

Aunt Tiffany smiled. "And I guess you're going to?"

"Well, maybe…" Abi said, ducking her head to look at the dogs, a little embarrassed to ask in front of Daisy, and unsure if her aunt would mind.

"I'll tell you what," Aunt Tiffany said. "Since you've been such a huge help today, I'm sure we can arrange for Emily to come and visit for a couple of days later in the summer. OK?"

Abi beamed. "That would be brilliant! Thanks, Aunt Tiffany!"

This was going to be the best summer ever!

Chapter Seven

The long pink car came to a stop outside a large building and the driver hopped out to open the door for them. Abi kept Lulu close on her lead as they jumped down and followed Daisy and Jade through the gleaming glass doors, Aunt Tiffany and Hugo behind them.

Abi hadn't ever been inside a TV studio, although she'd often wondered what it would be like. Still, she hadn't dreamed it could be so busy! As Daisy spoke to the receptionist, giving her Abi and Tiffany's names – as well as Lulu and Hugo's – Abi watched the people rushing past.

The receptionist waved them through and Daisy's high heels tip-tapped ahead of them down the long corridor. The dogs' claws clicked on the hard floor as they scampered after her too. Jade stayed close at Daisy's heels, while Hugo and Lulu dragged Aunt Tiffany and Abi after them in their excitement.

But the dogs didn't get very far. In their hurry, they weaved around each other so much that their leads got tangled! Abi set about untangling them quickly. Lulu whined and Hugo lay down on the floor, but Jade kept trying to get to Daisy.

Eventually, Abi got them untangled and they all carried on. The corridor reached a crossroads, and a girl with bright purple hair appeared, a clipboard in her hands.

"Sara! Hi," Daisy said. "These are my friends, Tiffany and Abi. Abi is going to be looking after Jade for me until it's time for us to go on. Can you show them around a bit?"

Sara ticked something off on her clipboard and nodded. "Sure. But you need to get to make-up right now, Miss Lane."

"On my way!" She handed Jade's lead to Abi and crouched down next to the tiny Pom Pom. "Now, you be a very good girl for Abi? I won't be gone long." She gave the dog a kiss on the top of her fluffy head.

"I'll look after her," Abi promised.

"I know you will." Daisy headed off down the corridor, lifting her hand over her head to wave them goodbye. "See you all soon!"

Jade yapped and started off after her owner, but Abi knelt down and put her hand on the little dog's back to keep her still. "You're staying with me for now, Jade. Remember?"

Jade sat down and, after a moment, the barking stopped.

"I can see why she left her with you," Sara

said. "Normally Jade's barking and running round trying to get to Daisy the whole time she's gone! Come on, I'll show you to the set. You can have a look around before we start filming, if you like."

"Yes, please!" Abi jumped up with excitement. A real TV set! Emily was never going to believe this.

They followed Sara through another maze of corridors, past people pushing rails full of sparkly outfits, and a room filled with people drinking coffee and reading scripts. Then Sara stopped by one door. It looked just like all the others, except for some lights on the wall.

Sara pushed it open and suddenly they were standing on the set of *Limelight!*

Aunt Tiffany was asking Sara questions about the show and the guests, with Hugo sat at her feet, but Abi was far more interested in

the set itself. She spotted the chair where Kerri
Kaye, the main presenter, sat every week. Abi
wondered if she might get to meet her!

And there was the co-host's chair, where Daisy would sit later, and the sofa where the guests sat. It felt strange, seeing something so familiar from the TV in real life.

Maybe she should prepare Jade, Abi thought. Daisy had been on the show before, but had Jade? If she knew where Daisy would be sitting, maybe Jade would be calmer during filming. "Look, Jade," Abi called, stepping up on to the stage set. "This is Daisy's chair."

She heard the clatter of claws on the hard floor behind her and, when she looked, Lulu and Jade had scampered up the few steps on to the stage and got their leads tangled again.

Abi sighed and set about untangling them. Maybe, now they were safely inside, she could take them off the leads… She looked over to where Aunt Tiffany was chatting with Sara. Should she ask? But she didn't want to interrupt and besides, Abi had done OK on her own so far.

She unclipped the leads from the glittery collars, and Jade and Lulu both set about exploring the set, snuffling around the furniture. Abi smiled. They were fine.

But then, somewhere behind them, a door slammed. Jade looked up, eyes wide and frightened.

"Don't worry," Abi said soothingly, like she'd heard her mum do with scared animals. But it was too late. A man yelled something over on the other side of the room and Jade was gone, racing across the stage, squeezing between two bits of set and disappearing into the maze of the TV studio beyond!

Chapter Eight

Abi's heart bumped against the inside of her chest as she raced across the set after Jade, with Lulu at her side. Where had Jade raced off to? She glanced over at Aunt Tiffany. She was still talking with Sara. With a bit of luck, Abi could get Jade back before anyone even noticed they were gone.

Abi felt in her pockets. She still had the Barker's Bites. She could use them to tempt Jade back. It would be easy!

Slipping behind the two large boards that were the pretend walls of the set, Abi whispered, "Jade? *Jade?*"

Lulu barked. Abi looked up and spotted an open door just in time to see Jade running through it. "*Jade!*"

But the little dog didn't stop.

"We have to catch up with her!" Abi said to Lulu, clipping her lead back on before they followed Jade through the door. Lulu kept up with Abi as she ran.

Through the door was another long corridor. Up ahead, Abi could see Jade scampering away. She was nearly at the end of the corridor where it split in two directions. After that Abi knew there would be more turnings, more open doors… Jade could go anywhere!

"We've got to catch her before she turns!" she panted, running faster. "Jade! I've got biscuits! Biscuits, Jade!" Abi called, but the dog didn't stop.

Jade only had little legs, Abi told herself. She couldn't run that fast. As long as Abi kept Jade in sight, she'd catch her eventually. She had to. Jade would get so upset if she didn't have Daisy *or* Abi with her!

Jade's claws scratched against the tiled floor as she flung herself left at the end of the corridor. Abi and Lulu followed, Abi almost banging into the wall as she raced round the corner. She was so nearly there, she could almost...

Abi dived, grabbing for Jade, but the dog squeezed through her hands, her tiny body slipping against Abi's fingers as she ducked under a table. Crash! Abi collided with the table and fell to the ground. Sheets of paper and plastic cups rained down around her head.

Jade barked loudly at the sudden noise and raced away out of sight, even faster than before!

"Oh no," Abi groaned, getting to her feet. "Where now? She could be anywhere!"

Lulu stood beside a slightly open door, nosing her way through.

"Did she go that way?" Abi asked, and Lulu barked.

"I hope that means yes," Abi said, pushing the door open all the way.

"*And our host tonight is…*" Abi's eyes widened. She knew that voice. She knew what came next. "*Danny Flame!*"

Abi stepped closer and the familiar sight of the *Fame or Flame?* quiz show came into view. There were the contestants at their podiums, and the lit-up wheel at the back with all the question categories on painted flames. And there was Danny Flame himself, grinning at the cameras. And there— Oh no! There was Jade, dashing across the stage!

Before she could stop her, Lulu was in hot pursuit, racing past the contestants and dragging Abi along behind her by her lead.

"Sorry!" Abi called as she chased both dogs round the contestants, who all looked very confused.

"Is this part of the game?" one of them asked.

"*What* is going on here?" yelled Danny Flame, as across the studio someone yelled, "Cut!"

Jade darted between the contestants' podiums again, barking loudly.

The poor thing had to be terrified! There were so many lights and noises and strange people, all talking at once.

Abi lurched forward again to grab Jade, but this time Lulu got in her way. Abi's feet left the floor as Lulu's fluffy, wriggly body brushed against her legs and Abi fell over, bashing into the Wheel of Fire.

"Ow!" she cried, as the Wheel of Fire wobbled, then toppled backwards with a crash! Jade yelped loudly and Abi looked around for her. Where had Jade disappeared to now?

Pushing herself up as she spotted her, Abi raced forward again, ignoring all the yelling and commotion as people crowded on to the stage to fix the Wheel of Fire. But as Abi got closer,

Jade jumped over the edge of the game-show set, landing on a big black lever. Suddenly a flurry of glitter and confetti rained down on to the set. One of the contestants shouted with surprise and Danny Flame started yelling again as his perfectly styled black hair was showered with sparkly bits.

"Abi? Are you in here?" Abi's eyes widened. That was Aunt Tiffany. If she found her here in this mess, without Jade … she'd never be trusted to help out at Pooch Parlour again!

"Abi!" Aunt Tiffany called and Abi ran after Jade as fast as she could, shaking glitter from her hair. She had to fix this!

Chapter Nine

Ignoring the calls and yells of the people following her, Abi chased Jade through the door out of the studio and into another long corridor. They all looked the same!

Abi could hear Lulu scampering along beside her, and she knew they had to be leaving a trail of glitter behind them, but she didn't look down. She couldn't risk taking her eyes off Jade for a moment!

Up ahead, Abi spotted another open door, this one with a large gold star on it. "Don't let her go in there. Please don't go in there," she muttered under her breath. A star like that on the door probably meant that a celebrity was inside. And she wasn't sure that all celebrities would be as nice as Daisy.

But Jade didn't seem worried. The little Pomeranian scrambled to a stop outside the door then darted inside. Just seconds behind, Abi rushed through the door too. Perhaps she could get Jade out before whoever was in the room noticed...

Too late.

Abi just managed to stop herself crashing into a dressing table full of glass bottles and make-up. Lulu slid to a halt under the table, right next to a pair of fluffy purple slippers that had been left there.

"Goodness. More visitors!" a woman exclaimed.

Abi recognized that voice. There, at the other end of the room, dressed in a long red dress and with her hair and make-up perfectly done, sat Kerri Kaye, star presenter of *Limelight!* And Jade was sitting in her lap!

"I assume you're looking for my friend here," Kerri said, running a hand over Jade's bushy coat. Jade, at least, had missed the glitter storm, since she'd been at the controls. Brushing glitter out of her thick coat would have taken ages!

Abi nodded, too nervous to speak. What would Kerri Kaye think of a nine-year-old girl with a runaway Pomeranian and a bichon frise who was sniffing her slippers?

Kerri leaned forward in her chair and Abi prepared to be yelled at. She'd promised Daisy she'd take care of Jade, and she hadn't.

"Are you all right?" Kerri asked softly, and tears stung at the back of Abi's eyes.

"I'm … I'm very sorry Jade ran in here. And Lulu. And, well, me." Abi swallowed. Still no shouting so far.

"Did this little mischief-maker get away from you?" Kerri asked, rubbing between Jade's ears.

Abi nodded again. "Daisy Lane asked me to look after her while she was having her make-up done, but Jade got spooked when we were looking at the *Limelight!* stage set and she ran off."

"And you chased after her?" Kerri asked.

"Yes," Abi said. "You see, I brought some Barker's Bites for her and I thought I could tempt her back with them. But she kept running and I couldn't get close enough. And then Danny Flame was yelling at us, and Jade set off the glitter machine, and I fell over and… I'm really, really sorry. Aunt Tiffany is going to be *so* mad."

Abi stared at the toes of her shoes, wishing she could just be safely back at Pooch Parlour again, looking through clothes with Mel, or helping bathe Lulu. Anywhere she didn't have glitter in her hair and confetti in her shoes.

Maybe she wasn't cut out for working with dogs after all…

But, to her amazement, Kerri started to smile, and then to laugh.

Perhaps Abi wasn't in quite as much trouble as she thought.

Jade jumped down from Kerri's lap and came to snuffle around Abi's ankles, as if to say she was sorry for running away.

"I don't mean to laugh," Kerri said, wiping her eyes. "It's just that Danny takes that show of his far too seriously. They probably weren't even filming – just rehearsing. And honestly, Jade has done much worse before."

"Really?" Abi hardly dared to believe it.

"Really," Kerri told her. "Last time Daisy and Jade came to see me here, one of our runners nearly ended up with a broken leg. Any visit from Jade that doesn't end with a trip to the hospital is a good one in my book. And anyway, she just wanted to come and see her friend Kerri, didn't you, darling?" Kerri slipped off her chair and got down on her knees, and Jade came running back towards her. "If ever she can't find Daisy, I'm the next best thing!"

"So … do you really think I might not be in trouble?"

Kerri smiled. "Seems to me that you did your very best to look after Jade and stick with her. And Daisy must think you've got a way with animals if she trusted you with Jade," she added, as Lulu reappeared from under the table and settled herself down at Abi's side.

"I love animals," Abi admitted. "When I grow up, I want to work with animals in TV and films."

"Then you're definitely in the right place," Kerri said. "However did you meet Daisy?"

"She brought Jade in to Pooch Parlour, my aunt's dog-grooming salon," Abi explained. "I'm helping out there for the summer."

"And you really think your aunt will be mad at you?"

"Abi? Abi!" Aunt Tiffany's voice echoed

down the corridor outside, and behind her Abi could hear more voices complaining and shouting.

She took a deep breath. "Looks like we're about to find out."

Chapter Ten

"Oh, Abi! There you are," Aunt Tiffany said as Abi and Kerri stepped out of the dressing room, Lulu and Jade beside them. "I was so worried! I followed your glitter trail all the way from the *Fame or Flame?* studio. You and Lulu left quite a mess behind you!"

"I'm sorry, Aunt Tiffany," Abi said, looking down at the floor. "I know it was my job to look after Jade, but she got scared when the door slammed, and took off. I was just trying to catch her."

"Which she did," Kerri added, putting an arm around Abi's shoulders.

Behind Aunt Tiffany, all the people who'd been following quietened down and went back to their jobs. Apparently if Kerri Kaye said Abi was all right, no one else could be mad!

"But she didn't have to do it all on her own," Aunt Tiffany said, looking at Abi.

Abi blushed. Maybe she should have asked Aunt Tiffany for help catching Jade, but she'd wanted to prove she could fix things herself!

Kerri looked thoughtful. "You know, I think I'd like to hear more about Pooch Parlour," she said. "I've got some time before filming starts. Why don't you come in and tell me about it, Tiffany? Abi, would you mind looking after the dogs for a little longer?"

Abi looked down at Lulu, Hugo and Jade, all staring up at her. "You three better behave," she told them, as she followed Kerri and Aunt

Tiffany inside. Then, clipping Jade back on to her lead, she pulled out the packet of Barker's Bites. The poor things must be hungry after their adventures!

As the dogs started to munch the biscuits, Abi looked at Lulu's coat, all sparkly with glitter and confetti, and sighed. Looked like she had another big job ahead of her that afternoon – brushing Lulu!

Later that evening, back at Aunt Tiffany's flat, Abi was curled up on the sofa with a cup of hot chocolate, two dogs snuggled next to her. Hugo was in his favourite tartan dressing gown again. Lulu, finally glitter-free after a lot of brushing, wore the purple T-shirt with ribbons that Abi had picked out that morning, along with the bright pink bow Aunt Tiffany had chosen for her.

"Are we ready?" Aunt Tiffany asked, settling down beside them with her own mug. She reached for the remote control and turned on the TV.

The screen lit up to show the *Limelight!* set, all ready for show time. As the cameras zoomed in, Abi sat up straighter, watching out for her new friends. There was Kerri, looking every bit as glamorous as she had in real life. And next to her...

"Look, there's Daisy!" Aunt Tiffany said.

"And Jade," Abi added, pointing at the little Pomeranian sitting beside Daisy in her matching cape and beret.

Aunt Tiffany smiled. "She looks wonderful. You did a really great job today, Abi. Even with Jade's adventures at the TV studio! But you should know you can always ask me for help when you need it."

Abi flushed, but her aunt smiled gently.

The opening music faded away, and Aunt Tiffany and Abi sat quietly to watch as the show started. But when one of the guests, famous chef and dog-lover, Felicity Bower, complimented Jade's outfit, Abi squealed.

This was the moment she'd been waiting for, the most exciting part of the whole show. And even though she knew what Daisy and Kerry were going to say, as she'd seen it during filming, she couldn't wait to watch it again.

"Doesn't she look great!" Daisy agreed, on screen. "And that's thanks to my friends Tiffany and Abi at Pooch Parlour, you know. I never take Jade anywhere else for her beauty treatments."

"And," Kerri added, "Tiffany is going to be on the show next week, talking about looking after the pets of the rich and famous, including the dogs belonging to the royal family of Monaco!"

Aunt Tiffany raised her hot-chocolate mug to Abi, and Abi clinked hers against it. But before they could drink, Aunt Tiffany's work phone rang.

"Hello, Pooch Parlour. Next Tuesday? I think we may have an opening…" Aunt Tiffany pulled the appointments book off the coffee table on to her lap. "How would eleven thirty suit you? Perfect." She hung up. "It looks like Jade's last-minute visit to Pooch Parlour might be good for business," she said, then laughed as the phone rang again.

Abi smiled. It seemed her first day hadn't been such a disaster after all. And it looked like business at Pooch Parlour would be booming all summer.

Abi couldn't wait!

Read an extract from

Dog Star

When Abi hears that Pooch Parlour will be the
official salon for a group of gorgeous dog stars, she is
thrilled! She will be grooming the most glamorous dogs
in town! But can Abi help a perky little Yorkie called
Pickle to get her big break? Pickle wants to shine!

"Come on, you two." Abi tugged lightly on the leads of the poodles. She was glad that Frosty and Sooty loved Pooch Palace's Doggy Daycare so much that they didn't want to leave, but it was time for them to go home to their owners!

Beside her, Abi's fluffy little bichon frise, Lulu, gave a small bark. Abi smiled. Lulu knew that once they'd delivered the poodles to Mr and Mrs Harris in reception, she'd get some Barker's Bites as a treat. No wonder she was in a hurry to get them moving.

"See you later, Abi." Rebecca, who ran the Doggy Daycare, waved at them as they left and the door swung shut behind them. Abi liked helping out at the Daycare. There were always lots of interesting new dogs to meet and fun games to play with them. Lulu liked it too – especially if one of the visiting dogs was in a playful mood. The Doggy Daycare had all the best toys – and Abi and Lulu had the whole summer to play with them, while they stayed with Aunt Tiffany.

With the Daycare out of sight, the poodles followed obediently at heel, and Lulu trotted along just behind. As Abi led them down the corridors of her aunt's luxury dog-grooming salon, she passed a few members of Pooch Palace staff. They all said hello and most stopped to pat Lulu on the head. Everyone knew how much Lulu liked to be petted.

"Oh, Abi. Great!" Kim bustled down the corridor towards them. "Can you do me a favour, if you're heading to reception? I have to take this message to your aunt, so can you keep an eye on the front desk? I'll be back in two minutes. If anyone comes in, just ask them to take a seat until I get back."

"Of course," Abi said. She pulled the curtain that led into reception to one side and let the dogs go first. Mr and Mrs Harris were already waiting, and Frosty and Sooty barked, rushing forward to greet them.

Abi handed their leads to Mrs Harris with a smile. "They've had a great time," she said.

"Oh, I'm so glad," Mrs Harris said. "I do worry when I have to leave them, but I know they're in good hands here at Pooch Palace."

Abi waved the Harrises off through the big front window of the salon. As soon as they turned the corner, Lulu placed her paws on Abi's leg, almost standing up, and Abi laughed. "Don't worry, Lulu, I haven't forgotten about your Barker's Bites! When Kim gets back, we'll go and find some."

Just then, the front door opened. Abi and Lulu headed to the reception desk and smiled at the newcomers – a tall man in jeans and a T-shirt, and a girl around Abi's age carrying a tiny Yorkshire terrier puppy.

"Welcome to Pooch Palace," Abi said politely.

The man raised his eyebrows. "Aren't you a little young to be working here?" he asked with a grin.

"I'm just helping out for the summer," Abi explained. "Kim – that's the receptionist – will be back any second." What else had Kim told her to say? Abi glanced round the room and spotted the long, velvet sofa beside the desk. That was it! "Would you like to take a seat until she gets back?"

"Actually, I have an appointment with

Tiffany," the man said, not sitting down. Instead, he started pacing round the reception area, picking up catalogues and leaflets, flicking through them quickly then putting them back down again. "My name is Don Francis. I'm a film director."

Abi's eyes widened. She knew that name! Don Francis was the director of the *Barking Mad* movies, starring Pooch Palace's most famous client, Daisy Lane. She wondered if Daisy had recommended them.

"And I'm Polly," the girl said, settling on to the sofa. "His daughter. And this is Pickle," she added, pointing at the Yorkie.

"I'm Abi and this is Lulu."

Lulu barked at her name and padded over to Pickle. The two little dogs sniffed round each other, darting back and forth, neither quite sure what to make of the other. Lulu had grown used to being round a lot of new dogs since they'd arrived at Pooch Palace, but Abi didn't know how well Pickle played with strangers.

She waited, a little nervously, until Lulu's tail began to wag, the whole back half of her body wiggling with excitement. Pickle's tail started to move too, and the tiny Yorkie yapped and nuzzled Lulu's side.

Abi smiled at Polly. "I'll just go and fetch Aunt Tiffany," she said, happy to leave Lulu with her new friend.

She rushed towards the curtain that led to the Pooch Palace offices, but paused before she went through. Turning round, she saw Mr Francis inspecting a display of dog brushes by the counter.

"Um, Mr Francis…" He looked up, and Abi took a breath. "I just wanted to say … I really love your films!"

The words came out in a rush, and Abi bit her lip as soon as she'd blurted them out. She shouldn't be bothering a famous film director!

But Mr Francis grinned at her. "Well, that's good news," he said, "because I'm making one just round the corner from here."

Abi gasped. "*Really?*" It was too exciting for words!

"Really," Mr Francis said with a nod. "It's called *Sally White and the Seven Dogs.* And what's more, I'm here today to see if we can use Pooch Palace for the dogs' grooming before we start filming!"

Read *Dog Star* to find out what happens next!

How to be a Pooch-Pampering Professional!

Dog grooming can be heaps of fun for both you and your pup – but it's important to know the right techniques!

Follow our top tips for the perfect pamper:

Make a Splash!

Some pooches love baths, but for others they can be a bit scary. Try giving your pup treats in the tub, so he or she connects water with having fun.

Brush Up!

A dog's coat needs brushing to keep it glossy. Even if your pup is short-haired like Hugo, regular brushing will help to remove loose dead hairs and keep your pooch's fur slick and clean so they look and feel their best.

Perfect Match!

Find out what kind of brush is right
for your breed of dog. A fluff-ball like
Jade needs a pin brush, whereas a curved
wire brush is best for Lulu's wavy fur.
Ask your breeder or local dog-grooming
parlour for advice.

Smooth Moves!

Sometimes a dog's fur can get tangled
into clumps called "mats", though regular
brushing will help prevent this. If your poor
pup's coat is matted, ask an adult to help you
rub some baby oil into the knots before very
gently combing them out with your fingers.

Natural Beauty!

Dogs come in a range of beautiful colours and it's
best to keep it that way! Dyeing a dog's fur can
cause an allergic reaction, making your pup very
uncomfortable. The staff at Pooch Palace never dye a
dog's fur – the pups are gorgeous just as they are!

Did you know...?
Fun facts about Pomeranians!

Queen Victoria owned several Pomeranian pups
and helped to make this breed of little dogs popular.

Pomeranians are descended from the Spitz
group of dogs that were used to pull sleds in Iceland.
Modern Poms are much smaller – they'd find
it very hard to pull a sledge!

The "cutest dog in the world" is a Pomeranian – he's
called Boo and has his own merchandise, including
mugs and lunch boxes!

A Pomeranian was one of the two dogs
rescued from the Titanic – it made it on to one
of the lifeboats with its owner!

A Pom Pom's tail is long and fluffy for a reason –
it keeps a Pom's nose warm while it's sleeping!

Read them all!

Pooch Parlour

V.I.P
(Very Important Pooch)

Katy Cannon

Pooch Parlour

Dog Star

Katy Cannon

Pooch Parlour

Passion for Fashion

Out in June

Katy Cannon

Katy Cannon was born in the United
Arab Emirates, grew up in North Wales
and now lives in Hertfordshire with her
husband and daughter Holly.

Katy loves animals, and grew up with a cat,
lots of fish and a variety of gerbils. One of
her favourite pastimes is going on holiday
to the seaside, where she can paddle in
the sea and eat fish and chips!

**For more about the author,
visit her website:**

www.katycannon.com

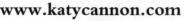